& Joshua Chaplinsky

Kanye West—
Reanimator

YOLO HOUSE PUBLISHERS
Melbourne + Boulder + Astoria

YOLO HOUSE PUBLISHERS

Melbourne + Boulder + Astoria

ISBN: 978-0-692-51612-6

Cover Art Copyright © 2015 by Dyer Wilk

Cover Design by Matthew Revert

Cover art based on the key art to the film
HP Lovecraft's Re-Animator

Interior Design by Cameron Pierce

Edited by Molly Tanzer

Printed in the USA.

Kanye West— Reanimator

I. From My Beautiful Dark Twisted Fantasy

Of Kanye West, who was my friend in college and after he dropped out, I can speak only with extreme sadness. This dysphoria is not due altogether to the sickening manner of his recent disappearance, but was engendered by the whole nature of his life-work, and first gained its acute form more than twenty years ago, when we were in the first year of our course at the Chicago State University in Illinois. While he was with me, the wonder and diabolism of his musical experiments fascinated me utterly, and I was his closest companion. (Some would say too close. There was much speculation regarding the nature of our partnership, but Kanye was a very private person and I didn't dare betray his confidence.) Now that we are no longer friends and the spell is broken, my side of the story can finally be told. The actual pain is far greater now than it was then. Memories and possibilities are ever more melancholic than the realities.

The first horrible incident of our acquaintance was the greatest shock I ever experienced, and it is only with reluctance that I repeat it. If not for Kanye's current status as a missing person, I would never dare. Otherwise the mere telling might result in litigation. Kanye had been known to slap a suit, and we ain't talking about Versace, either.

As I have stated, it started when we were in school where Kanye had already made himself notorious as a petulant young go-getter. His grandiose aspirations, which were widely ridiculed by the faculty and by his fellow-students, hinged on the narcissistic attention he paid his own career. In his experiments with sped-up vocal samples he started to make a name for himself, making music for other artists. Several times he had actually contributed guest verses to other rappers' tracks, but he soon saw that the perfection of his process, if indeed possible, would necessarily involve him embarking on a solo career. It likewise became clear that, since this endeavor would not allow time for his studies, he would have to disappoint his mother and abandon his education. Being an inveterate mama's boy, Kanye rarely if ever went against his mother's wishes. "You can't spell matriculation without matriarch," he would tell me. "Yes you can," I would reply.

I had always been exceptionally tolerant of Kanye's pursuits, and we frequently discussed his musical inspirations, whose ramifications and corollaries were almost infinite. Holding with purists that the so-called hip-hop scene was wallowing in a mire of cookie-cutter pop and gangsta rap, my friend believed that reanimation of the dead genre was still possible. It all depended on the receptiveness of the listener, not the critics, and unless actual decomposition had set in, a person fully equipped with a functioning brain would with suitable measures be set going again down that peculiar road towards "good taste." Kanye fully realised that were he to become the reagent which would restore vitality to the moribund scene he would require extreme freshness in his samples, and would have to inject his very soul into each track. It was this assertion which made his critics so carelessly sceptical, for they felt that true death had not occurred in the mainstream scene. But their opinion of Kanye would soon change.

It was not long after the detractors had interdicted his work that Kanye confided in me his resolution to get his music on the radio by any means necessary, all while he continued in secret the recording of his debut album. To hear him discussing ways and means of acquiring samples was rather inspiring, for at the college we had never procured samples outside the radio station's library. Whenever the local record stores proved inadequate, Kanye's posse (me) attended to this matter, and frequently made road trips to scour swap meets and go diggin' in the crates. Kanye was then a small, slender youth with strong features, a tight fade, piercing dark eyes, and a supple voice, and it was uncanny to hear him dwelling on the relative merits of obscure soul records by the likes of Maxine Brown and Baby Washington.

I was by this time his active and enthralled assistant — some would say too enthralled — and was the first to hear all his musical arrangements. I even contributed on occasion. In fact, it was I who suggested sampling "I Miss You" by Harold Melvin & the Blue Notes on "This Can't Be Life." I realize now I should have lobbied for a producer credit.

The song's popularity earned Kanye a position as an in-house producer for Roc-A-Fella Records, where he produced multiple tracks on Jay-Z's now classic album, *The Blueprint*. Yet he was still thought of predominantly as a producer and no one wanted to take a chance and give him a record deal as a rapper. After much pestering, then Roc-A-Fella head Damon Dash finally relented so that he wouldn't lose Kanye's expertise behind the boards. Production on *The College Dropout* commenced shortly thereafter.

We moved into a deserted farmhouse not far from Spahn Ranch, the old Manson family haunt, where we fitted up on the ground floor a control room and a vocal booth, each with dark curtains to conceal our midnight doings. The place was far from any road, and in sight of no other house, yet Kanye insisted these precautions were necessary. He had become increasingly secretive, and was paranoid that rumours of strange noises, started by chance nocturnal roamers, would soon bring disaster on our enterprise. It was agreed to call the whole thing a yogurt retreat if discovery should occur. I assumed he meant yoga, but no, he was adamant. Yogurt. Gradually we equipped our makeshift studio with materials either purchased in L.A. or quietly borrowed from Roc-A-Fella — materials secreted away in a Louis Vuitton backpack under watchful eyes — and stockpiled blank CDs for the many mixes we should have to make.

We were up all hours like meth heads, for Kanye's production demanded particular qualities. What these qualities were, he refused to say. He was obsessed with owls at the time and would wander the property early in the morning before the sun rose to collect owl pellets. He called them "nocturnal emissions" and insisted that be the working title of the album, so I was forced to explain to him the true meaning of the term. As a good Christian boy he had been admonished against self-abuse, and revealed his mother had called the result of said activity "lust tears."

Most people are familiar with the story of how Kanye broke his jaw. He was on an impromptu burrito run late one night during a particularly grueling recording session and got into a near-fatal motor-car accident not far from the studio. What they don't know is that this accident involved an oncoming vehicle whose operator was instantly killed. Before Kanye could succumb to the soothing grope of unconsciousness, he somehow managed to limp back to the studio and enlist my help. Thankfully the other vehicle was still drivable. I drove off with car and corpse and stashed them both in one of our many barns. The property had at least half a dozen dilapidated barns. One of Kanye's weird stipulations was the amount of barns the studio required. "This is at least a four-barn record," he was quoted as saying. I believe the idea came from the mishearing of a line in an old Dave Chappelle sketch in which the Wu-Tang Clan played financial advisors. "You need to diversify yo barns, nigga!" Kanye really took that advice to heart.

Kanye returned to his vehicle to wait for the ambulance, where he lost consciousness. He later told me he dreamt he was Evel Knievel, riding a jet-propelled phallus into the yawning gap of the Grand Canyon, and had his first wet dream. I refused once again to allow him to name the album *Nocturnal Emissions*. When the paramedics arrived, he informed them he had fallen asleep at the wheel and collided with a tree. How they swallowed such an obvious lie I will never understand. There are those who believe Kanye signed his soul over to the devil that night, his released essence the ink and his dream the contract. They cite the subsequent take-off of his career as proof. All I know is, Kanye had finally "discovered" himself. We went through sixty-three boxes of tissues during the recording of "Through the Wire." That's a lot of ink. He also drank two hundred and thirty-seven milkshakes. Kanye refused to list me as co-producer on the song, but I was given a "Procurer of Milkshakes" credit in the liner notes, which was nice.

The driver of the other motor-car was a skinny young bohemian and Kanye was wracked with guilt at the thought of being responsible for snuffing out such beauty. (I personally did not see what all the fuss was about. The kid wasn't *that* good looking.) He decided that since his music could reanimate dead careers, why not the literal human dead?

It was a repulsive task, but I was blinded by loyalty and admiration. The affair made us rather nervous, especially the stiff form and vacant face of the deceased, but we managed. On an improvised dissecting-table in barn number three, by the light of a laptop computer, the specimen was not quite as handsome looking. It had been a sturdy and apparently unimaginative youth of the plebeian type — horn-rimmed glasses, skinny-leg jeans — a sound animal without psychological subtleties, and probably having vital processes of the simplest and healthiest sort. Most likely not a true hip-hop fan. Now, with the eyes closed, it looked more asleep than dead.

Looking back, I recognize this as Kanye's first true test as an artist — a confrontation with real-life death. Here was an individual ready to be called back from the grave by Kanye's music, like

Lazarus from the tomb. The tension on our part became very great. We knew that there was scarcely a chance for anything like complete success, and could not avoid hideous fears at possible grotesque results of partial animation. Especially were we apprehensive concerning the mind and impulses of the creature, since during the accident some of the more delicate cerebral cells might well have suffered damage. Kanye, being a good Christian boy with a burgeoning god complex — purported deal with the devil notwithstanding — still held some curious notions about the traditional "soul" of man, and felt an awe at the secrets that might be told by one returning from the dead. He wondered what sights this placid youth might have seen in inaccessible spheres, and what the man could relate if fully restored to life. Kanye was calmer than I as he forced the pin-shaped plug of a music cable into a vein on the body's arm, plugging the other end into his laptop. He hit play on "Keep the Receipt", which would later be cut from the album, due in part to the events that followed. The track featured a brilliant, crack-fueled performance by Ol' Dirty Bastard (aka ODB, aka Dirt McGirt, aka Big Baby Jesus, may he rest in piece), and I think cutting it was an insult to the man.

The waiting was gruesome, but Kanye never faltered. Every now and then he applied his ear to the chest of the specimen, and bore the negative results in typical Kanye fashion: by throwing a fit and going on a non-sequitur rant. He'd wax hyperbolic about the breadth and width of his art, claiming it couldn't be contained by mere genre conventions like "life." After about three-quarters of an hour without the least sign of life he disappointedly pronounced the track we were using inadequate, but decided to make the most of the opportunity and try one change in the mix before disposing of his ghastly prize. We had that afternoon dug a grave in the cellar, and would have to fill it by dawn — for although we had fixed a lock on the barn, we wished to shun even the remotest risk of a ghoulish discovery. Besides, the body would not be even approximately fresh the next night and Kanye claimed the most sensitive of olfactories. If a particularly fetid patch of air wafted into his vicinity he would grimace and proclaim, "There sure are a lot of smells floating around the ol' factory." So taking the laptop back into the control room, we left our silent guest on the slab in the dark, and bent every energy to the remixing of the track; the panning and the levels supervised by

Kanye with an almost fanatical care.

The awful event was very sudden, and wholly unexpected. I was tweaking a filter on one of the plug-ins and Kanye was busy smoking a blunt on the toilet when from the pitch-black barn we had left there burst the most appalling and daemoniac succession of sounds that either of us had ever heard (this was pre-*808s & Heartbreak*, mind you). Not more unutterable could have been the chaos of hellish sound if the pit itself had opened to simultaneously release the careers of both 95 South *and* Tag Team, for in one inconceivable cacophony was centered all the supernal terror and unnatural despair of animate nature. Human it could not have been — it is not in man to make such sounds — and without a thought of our possible discovery, both Kanye and I leaped to the nearest window like stricken animals; he with his pants around his ankles, dropping his lit blunt on the carpet and overturning tables and lamps, vaulting madly into the starred abyss of the rural night. I think he shit himself as we stumbled frantically toward town, though as we reached the outskirts we put on a semblance of restraint — just enough to seem like belated revellers staggering home from a debauch. Revellers who had possibly shit themselves.

We did not separate, but managed to get to a motel, where we whispered with the lights on until dawn, like girls at a slumber party. By then we had calmed ourselves a little with rational theories and plans for investigation, so that we could sleep through the day — work for once being disregarded. But that next day two items in the paper, wholly unrelated, made it again impossible for us to sleep. The old farmhouse had inexplicably burned to an amorphous heap of ashes; that we could understand because of the errant, unattended blunt. Also, the young bohemian's car was found some 20 miles from us, empty, radio tuned to a local hip-hop station. That we could not understand. The incident, however, partially inspired the lyrics to, "Jesus Walks." (The rest of which were inspired by Kanye's love of Adam Sandler movies.)

For years afterwards Kanye would look frequently over his shoulder and complain of fancied footsteps behind him. It explains his apparent disdain for the paparazzi and distrust of the media, although it does not explain his flirtation with the spotlight via assimilation into the Kardashian clan. Fans chocked it up to him being an eccentric creative, but I alone bore the burden of truth. Regardless, *The College Dropout* was a huge success, and though no one but

Kanye knew it at the time (he was nothing if not confident — some would say too confident), it was just the beginning of a long and turbulent career.

II. The Plague-Damon

I shall never forget that hideous autumn all those years ago, when like a noxious effluvia invading the ol' factory, "Hey Ya!" by Outkast overtook the airwaves. It is by that syrupy scourge the mainstream music press recall the year, for truly it inspired miasma in lovers of real hip-hop; yet for me there is a greater horror associated with that time — a horror known to me alone now that Kanye West has disappeared.

Kanye and I were balls-deep in the recording of *The College Dropout*, after we ourselves had dropped out of Chicago State University, and my friend had attained a wide notoriety because of his efforts leading toward the revivification of the hip-hop scene. After the production of uncounted tracks for Roc-A-Fella Records, Kanye stopped taking gigs so that he could record his debut in a rundown farmhouse in the desert, and had on one terrible and unforgettable occasion killed (vehicularly manslaughtered?) a person in a car accident and taken the body back to one of the diverse barns on the property.

I was with him on that odious occasion, and saw him insert into the still veins a cable connected to his laptop, the air between us charged with a subtle eroticism. Kanye hit play on a funky work-in-progress, which he thought would inject some soul into the corpse and restore life's processes. It had ended horribly — in a delirium of shit and fear which we gradually came to attribute to our own overwrought nerves — and Kanye had never afterward been able to shake off the maddening sensation of being haunted and hunted by the public. According to him, the track had not been quite fresh enough; it was obvious that to restore normal mental attributes to a body the track in question must be some next level shit; and the burning of the farmhouse had prevented us from burying the thing. It would have been better if we could have known it was underground.

After that experience Kanye had discontinued his creative efforts for some time; but as the zeal of the born artist slowly returned, he again became impassioned with finishing *The College Dropout*, pleading for the use of the Roc-A-Fella recording studios, as well as, to my dismay, fresh human specimens for him to try to revive. For he had latched onto a new way to save hip-hop from the perpetual doldrums of mainstream entertainment: resurrecting The Notorious B.I.G. and Tupac. In Kanye's mind, the three of them would comprise the Holy Trinity of hip-hop, and usher in a new era of creative enlightenment.

His pleas, however, were wholly in vain; for the decision of Damon Dash was inflexible, and the other executives all endorsed the verdict of their leader. In the radical theory of the reanimation of the hip-hop scene, they continued to indulge Kanye, but in the radical theory of reanimation of actual dead persons, regardless of how iconic, they saw nothing but the immature vagaries of a youthful enthusiast whose slight form, tight fade, dark eyes, and soft voice gave no hint of the supernormal — almost diabolical — ego of the cold brain within. Besides, argued Dash, neither Biggie nor Tupac had any affiliation with Roc-A-Fella, so what benefit could it possibly have for them? Even in death, the duo were contractually bound to Badboy and Death Row Records, respectively.

And no one in their right mind wanted to fuck with Suge "Cuddle-Britches" Knight, even before he started running people over.

Kanye clashed disagreeably with Dash over the decision. I can see Kanye now as he was then — and I shiver. He grew pouty of face, but never backed down. He rebutted with a wordy dispute that did less credit to himself than to the kindly label head. He felt that he was needlessly and irrationally retarded in a supremely great work; Dash felt that Kanye was just needlessly and irrationally retarded. It was a work which Kanye could of course conduct to suit himself in later years, but which he wished to begin while still possessed of the exceptional facilities of the record label. That the tradition-bound executives should ignore his singular musical results, and persist in their denial of the possibility of reanimation of the literal dead in addition to the figuratively dead, was inexpressibly disgusting and almost incomprehensible to a youth of Kanye's illogical temperament. Only greater maturity (which he did not possess) could help him understand the chronic mental limitations of the "record-executive" type — the product of generations of pathetic capitalists; attentive and sometimes encouraging when you didn't rock the boat and were lining their pockets; yet always narrow, intolerant, custom-ridden, and lacking in perspective. Age has more charity for these incomplete yet high-souled characters, whose worst real vice is timidity, and who are ultimately punished by general ridicule for turning art into business — people like Quincy Jones, Phil Spector, Brian Eno, Rick Rubin, Butch Vig, and every sort of innovator turned success, which Kanye would also eventually become. Kanye, young despite his marvellous creative achievements, had scant patience with Damon Dash and his executives; and nursed an increasing resentment, coupled with a desire to prove his theories to these obtuse veterans in some striking fashion. Like most youths, he indulged in elaborate daydreams of revenge, triumph, and final magnanimous forgiveness. He truly was a drama queen.

And then had come the scourge: "Hey Ya!", infectious and saccharine, from half of the collective mind known as Outkast. Kanye had finished recording on *The College Dropout* about the time of its beginning, but had remained to finish mixing the album, so we were in the studio when it broke with full daemoniac fury upon the radio. Though Kanye was not yet an international superstar, "Through the Wire" was a hit and "Slow Jamz" featuring Jamie Foxx and Twista was about to be released, and he was pressed frantically into the public eye as his notoriety grew. But the "Hey Ya!" situation was almost past management, and requests ensued too frequently for the local radio stations to fully handle. More deserving singles were passed over, and even the iTunes servers were crammed with the material of unplayed artists. This circumstance was not without effect on Kanye, who thought often of the irony of the situation — so many dope singles, yet none of them were getting airplay! When you keep on diminishing art and not respecting the craft and smacking people in the face after they deliver monumental feats of music, it's disrespectful to inspiration.

He was afraid the same would happen to his music, and the terrific mental and nervous strain made my friend brood morbidly. If Kanye was anything, he was a brooder. Roc-A-Fella employees nicknamed him "Mother Hen" he brooded so much. They never called him such to his face, of course. Lesser-thans knew better than to incur the wrath of Kanye. Less creative personnel kept with the poultry motif by simply calling him, a cock.

But Kanye's gentle enemies at the label were

no less harassed with saving hip-hop, an endeavor which in turn had become about saving themselves. Roc-A-Fella had all but closed, and every producer and artist on the payroll was helping to fight the "Hey Ya!" plague. Damon Dash in particular had distinguished himself in sacrificial service, applying his extreme skill with whole-hearted energy to artists which many other labels shunned because of lack of talent. Before a month was over the fearless Dash had become a popular hero, putting out numerous shitty pop-rap records, though he seemed unconscious of his fame as he struggled to keep from collapsing with physical fatigue and nervous exhaustion. Kanye could not withhold admiration for the fortitude of his foe, but because of this was even more determined to prove to him the truth of his amazing doctrines. Taking advantage of the disorganisation of Roc-A-Fella, he managed to get a recently deceased body smuggled into the recording studio one night, and in my presence played it what would be *The College Dropout*'s third single, "All Falls Down". The wretched thing actually opened its eyes, but only stared at the ceiling with a look of soul-petrifying horror before collapsing into an inertness from which nothing could rouse it. Kanye said the track was not fresh enough. (He would remix it at least a dozen times before it was released.) That time we were almost caught before we disposed of the body, and Kanye doubted the advisability of repeating his daring misuse of the Roc-A-Fella studios.

The nature of the epidemic changed come August, when Usher took over the charts for months with "Yeah!", "Burn", and "Confessions Part II". Kanye and I were almost dead, and Dash did die, from exhaustion. The label employees all attended the hasty funeral and bought an impressive wreath, though the latter was quite overshadowed by the tributes sent by wealthy execs from other, more prosperous labels — specifically LaFace and Arista. It was almost as if they were rubbing their victory in Damon's dead face. After the funeral we were all somewhat depressed, and spent the afternoon at a bar; where Kanye, though shaken by the death of his champion/chief opponent, chilled Jay-Z and I with references to his notorious theories. Most of the mourners went home, or to various duties, as the evening advanced; but Kanye persuaded me to aid him in "making a night of it." Kanye's neighbors saw us arrive at his place about two in the morning, with a third man between us; and it appeared that we had evidently dined and wined rather well.

Their suspicions were erroneously confirmed; for about 3 a.m. they were aroused by cries coming from Kanye's, where when they broke down the door, they found the two of us unconscious on the blood-stained carpet, beaten, scratched, and mauled, and with the broken remnants of Kanye's laptop around us. Only an open window told what had become of our assailant, and many wondered how he himself had fared after the terrific leap from the second story which he must have made. There were some strange garments in the room, but Kanye upon regaining consciousness said they did not belong to the stranger, but were samples produced for his upcoming menswear line. He declared them subpar and ordered them burned as soon as possible in the capacious fireplace. To the police we both declared ignorance of our late companion's identity. He was, Kanye nervously said, just a G from around the way we had met at a bar of uncertain location. We had all been rather jovial, and Kanye and I did not wish to have our pugnacious companion hunted down. The cops seemed to buy our story, although we were on the receiving end of many a raised eyebrow.

That same night saw the beginning of the second horror — the horror that to me eclipsed the plague of such exclamatory songs as "Hey Ya!" and "Yeah!". The offices of LaFace Records were the scene of a terrible killing; a security guard having been clawed to death in a manner not only too hideous for description, but raising a doubt as to the human agency of the deed. Dawn revealed the unutterable thing. The manager of a bodega down the road was questioned, but he swore that no such beast had at any time browsed his wares. Those who found the body noted a trail of blood leading out of LaFace, to a small pool of red on the concrete just outside the bodega. A fainter trail led away from the establishment, but it soon gave out.

The next night Usher danced on the airwaves and unnatural madness howled in the wind. Through the fevered town had crept a curse which some said was greater than the pop-rap plague, and which some whispered was the embodied daemon-soul (or was it Damon-soul?) of the plague itself. Eight record stores were entered by a nameless thing which strewed red death in its wake — in all, seventeen maimed and shapeless remnants of bodies were left behind by the voice-less, sadistic monster that crept abroad. A few persons had half seen it in the dark, and said it was a well-dressed, bald-headed anthropomorphic fiend. It had not left behind quite all that it had attacked, for sometimes it had been hungry. The number it had killed was fourteen.

On the third night frantic bands of searchers, led by the police, captured it in an apartment near the Roc-A-Fella offices. They had organised the quest with care, keeping in touch by means of walkie talkie, and when someone had reported hearing a scratching at a shuttered window, the net was quickly spread. On account of the general alarm and precautions, there were only two more victims, and the capture was effected without major casualties. The thing was finally stopped by a bullet, though not a fatal one, and was rushed to the local hospital amidst universal excitement and loathing.

For it had been a man. This much was clear despite the nauseous eyes, the voiceless simianism, and the daemoniac (Damonic?) savagery. They dressed its wound and carted it to a mental health facility, where it beat its bald head against the walls of a padded cell for years to come — until the recent mishap, when it escaped under circumstances that few like to mention. What had most disgusted the searchers was the thing they noticed when the monster's face was cleaned — the mocking, unbelievable resemblance to a noted and successful record executive who had been entombed mere days before — the late Damon Dash, owner and label head of Roc-A-Fella Records.

To the vanished Kanye West and I the disgust and horror were supreme. I shudder tonight as I think of it; shudder even more than I did that morning when Kanye muttered through his bandages, "Damn it, the track wasn't quite fresh enough!"

III. Fifteen (More) Shots for Biggie

It is uncommon to empty the clip of a nine-millimeter handgun with great suddenness when one bullet would probably be sufficient, but many things in the life of Kanye West were uncommon. It is, for instance, not often that a young rapper leaving college is obliged to conceal the principles which guide his selection of beats and samples, yet that was the case with Kanye. After the success of *The College Dropout*, he was determined to procure the remains of both Biggie and Tupac for reanimation, despite the objections of Roc-A-Fella and despite their condition. The bodies of both men were known to have been cremated after their deaths and the ashes bequeathed to the families. Afeni Shakur, Tupac's mother, had moved to Georgia to start The Tupac Amaru Shakur Center for the Arts, and was infamously reclusive due to her former life as a member of the Black Panther Party. It was also alleged that Tupac's ashes had been rolled up and smoked by his crew, The Outlawz. Voletta Wallace, mother of The Notorious B.I.G., had moved to L.A. when her son became successful, and had stayed on afterwards to give interviews and conduct a feud with Lil' Kim, so we started there since it was close to home. In the meantime, we set up shop in a trio of Hollywood recording studios (so no one could know exactly where Kanye was at any given moment) and began work on Kanye's sophomore effort, *Late Registration*, with lily-white composer Jon Brion.

Outwardly Kanye was an artist only, but beneath the surface were aims of far greater and more terrible ambition — for the essence of Kanye's existence was a quest amid black and forbidden realms of the unknown, in which he hoped to uncover the secret of life and restore to perpetual animation the hip-hop scene. Such a quest demands strange materials, among them fresh tracks and fresh human bodies; and in order to keep supplied with the latter one must live quietly, which is why Kanye shunned the public.

Kanye and I had met in college, and I had been the only one to recognize the genius within him.

Gradually I had come to be his inseparable assistant — some would say too inseparable — and now that we had dropped out of college we continued to keep together.

It was easy to secure an audience with Voletta Wallace, as by this point Kanye was a huge star and she was always looking for producers for Biggie's myriad posthumous releases. But we bided our time. We purposefully chose recording studios with the greatest care, seizing at last on the aforementioned but unnamed three: The Record Plant, Chalice, and Grandmaster. They were situated in areas far from the suburbs. The distance from Voletta's was greater than we wished, but we could get no nearer studios without being in a more populated area. It was more important we be able to conduct our experiments undisturbed.

Work on *Late Registration* was unsurprisingly busy from the very first — busy enough to please the record label, and busy enough to prove distracting to Kanye, whose real interest lay in reanimating Biggie. Jon Brion, despite having never produced a hip-hop record before, had a lot in common with Kanye, musically, and the two hit it off. Some would say a little too off, and I must admit, it made me rather jealous. He was constantly luring Kanye in with a new song snippet, a new production tweak, distracting him from the secret laboratories we had fitted up in each studio — each with a long table under fluorescent lights, where in the small hours of the morning we prepared to plug Kanye's various compositions into the ashen remains of Biggie. Kanye was experimenting madly to find a beat which would start man's vital motions anew after they had been stopped by the thing we call death, but had encountered the most ghastly obstacles. Namely, Brion's non-hip-hop influences, dalliances with which Kanye was becoming increasingly enamored. He began to believe he wasn't out to save just hip-hop, but all of popular music.

Still, the tracks had to be exceedingly fresh, or the state of Biggie's remains would render perfect reanimation impossible. Indeed, the greatest problem was predicting what form the ashes would take — and if we should take it upon ourselves to mold them into a reasonable facsimile of the deceased rapper. In the end it was decided to let Biggie dictate his own form, as he was rather corpulent in life and there would be precious little ash. Ever since our first daemoniac session in the deserted farmhouse (and the following Damonic one), we had felt a brooding menace; and Kanye, though a calm, steely-eyed musical automaton in most respects, often confessed to a shuddering sensation of stealthy pursuit. He half felt that he was followed, a psychological delusion of his current popularity, enhanced by the undeniably disturbing fact that at least one of our reanimated specimens was still alive — a frightful carnivorous thing in a padded cell in Los Angeles. Then there was another — our first, from the farmhouse — whose exact fate we had never learned.

We had not been recording more than a few weeks when we could put off Voletta no longer. So one night, we paid her a surprise visit. She was confused but happy to oblige us. She set about making tea while we cased the joint for the notorious A.S.H.E.S., which, unfortunately, were not prominently displayed.

Kanye excused himself under the guise of nature's call and disappeared into the farther reaches of the house. It was left to me to make small talk with Voletta. Yes, progress on the new record was going swimmingly, I assured her. Of course Kanye would have time to set music to a handful of throwaway Biggie verses. Biggie was a legend, after all.

It was then that we were interrupted by the most girlish of shrieks followed by a cacophonous crash.

I leaped from my seat and followed Voletta as she headed off towards the source of the disruption. In her bedroom we found Kanye, hands covering his mouth to prevent any further squeals, a pile of ceramic shards and ash at his feet.

It took much damage control, but I managed to calm both the poor woman and the stricken Kanye. The bulk of the ashes were salvageable and I promised her a nice new urn, personally inscribed by Kanye, to replace the one that was broken. I also promised, in a stroke of genius if I may be so immodest, to take some of the ashes and have them pressed into the vinyl of a limited run of twelve-inch singles when Biggie's new-old record dropped (a practice that was catching on with vinyl enthusiasts in those days). It would ensure that this was literally a Biggie record and would make for an extravagant collector's item, copies of which we would furnish her free of charge, of course.

We carried home our allotment of Biggie in a plastic sandwich baggie. The Biggie Baggie, we called it. We approached the studio (I can't even remember which one. Whichever one Brion wasn't entertaining whores in that evening) from the alley in the rear, took the specimen in the back door and prepared it for the experiment. Our fear of discovery was absurdly great, though we had timed our trip to avoid the solitary security guard who patrolled the area. To add to our worry, we only had what amounted to about five ounces of Biggie. We mixed him with some water and flour — Kanye's idea, to add thickness — and poured him into a Hug Me the Bear ice cream cake mold Kanye had stolen from a local Carvel and claimed was a prototype for his Dropout Bear line of frozen treats.

The result was wearily anticlimactic. Ghastly as our prize appeared, the gloppy solution was wholly unresponsive to every track we played for it. Not even "Gold Digger", with its buoyant beat and Ray Charles sample, could provoke a reaction. So as the hour grew dangerously near to dawn, we did as we had done with the others — disposed of it, although this time it was a much simpler endeavor. We dumped the thing into the toilet and flushed. Or so I thought.

In retrospect, I should have never left it to Kanye to flush the toilet. This was a simple responsibility he could not be trusted with. He held fast to the old hippie axiom, *if it's yellow, let it mellow*, claiming that until the United States caught up to places like Europe and Japan when it came to toilet bowl technology, and imposed the mandatory implementation of a dual flush function on all toilet manufacturers, distinctly differentiating between "number ones" and "dirty twosies" as he called them, he would fight the good fight and refuse to waste water disposing of non-solids. I guess our Biggie concoction didn't qualify as solid in Kanye's eyes. Still, the mixture wasn't there the following morning.

But we didn't have time for that. The next day we were increasingly apprehensive about yet another source of worry. One of the more portly studio assistants had become hysterical over his missing child — a lass of five who had strayed off early during Bring Your Daughter to Work Day and failed to reappear — and had developed symptoms highly alarming in view of an already weak heart. It was a very foolish hysteria, for the child had often been misplaced before; the father was an exceedingly poor guardian. About seven o'clock in the evening he had died of cardiac arrest, and his frantic wife had made a frightful scene in her efforts to attack Kanye, whom she wildly blamed for not saving her husband's life, despite the fact that Kanye had been heating up a microwave corn dog in the studio kitchen at the time of the man's death. The staff had restrained the woman when she drew a kitchen knife from her purse, and Kanye departed amidst her inhuman shrieks, curses and oaths of vengeance. In her latest affliction the woman seemed to have forgotten her child, who was still missing as the night advanced. There was some talk of searching the alleys around the studio, but most of the family's friends were busy with the dead husband and the screaming woman. Altogether, the nervous strain upon Kanye must have been tremendous. Thoughts of police searching the studio and of the remains of the Biggie Pudding weighed heavily on his mind.

We retired around eleven, but I did not sleep well. We had taken to sleeping on the studio couches and they were not very comfortable. I was also preoccupied. L.A. had a surprisingly good police force, especially when it came to convicting black people, and I could not help fearing the mess which would ensue if the affair of the night before were ever tracked down. It might mean the end of all our work — and perhaps prison for both Kanye and myself (although the idea of us having nothing to keep us occupied but each other's company had its appeal). The clock had struck three and the moon shone in my eyes, but I turned over without rising to pull down the shade. Then came the knocking. Then came the whispers from Kanye.

I lay still and somewhat dazed, but before long I felt Kanye's moist breath as he again whispered, this time right in my ear. I turned to face him and we were nose to nose. He was clad in dressing-gown and bunny slippers, and had in his hands a nine-millimeter and an electric toothbrush. From the nine I knew he was thinking more of the crazed woman than of the police. From the toothbrush I didn't know what to think.

"There's someone at the door," he said. "It wouldn't do not to answer it, and it may be an employee anyway — it would be just like one of those fools to forget their wallet."

So we both went on tiptoe, with a fear partly justified and partly caused by the weird small hours. When we reached the door I cautiously unbolted it and threw it open, and as the moon streamed revealingly down on the form silhouetted there, Kanye did a peculiar thing. Despite the obvious danger of attracting notice and bringing down on our heads the dreaded police investigation — a thing which after all was mercifully averted by the relative isolation of the studio — my friend suddenly, excitedly, and unnecessarily emptied the entire clip of his nine-millimeter into the nocturnal visitor.

For that visitor was neither forgetful employee nor policeman. Looming hideously against the spectral moon was a gigantic misshapen thing not to be imagined save in nightmares — a bug-eyed, ash-grey apparition, covered with sewage and fecal matter and caked with blood, and having between its glistening teeth a snow-white, terrible, cylindrical object terminating in a tiny hand.

IV. The Scream of the Auto-Tune

Auto-Tune is what led me to doubt Kanye's genius, a doubt which harassed the latter years of our companionship. It is natural that such a thing as Auto-Tuned vocals should cause a musical connoisseur to become annoyed, for it is obviously not a pleasing or ordinary sound. I was used to hearing it on all sorts of shitty T-Pain songs, but its incorporation into Kanye's oeuvre was truly disheartening.

Kanye West, whose associate and confidant I was, possessed musical interests far beyond the usual purview of your average rapper. That was why, when recording *Late Registration*, he had chosen a group of isolated studios away from any residential area. Obviously more than music-making was taking place. Briefly and brutally stated, Kanye's sole absorbing interest used to be the reanimation of the hip-hop scene, which led to an absorbing interest in the reanimation of the dead. For this ghastly experimentation it was necessary to have a constant supply of fresh tracks and access to human bodies. In his mind, Kanye had never fully succeeded in reanimating a corpse because he had never been able to produce a track sufficiently fresh. What he wanted were beats from which vitality oozed, and bodies capable of receiving again the impulse toward that mode of motion called life. There was hope that this second and artificial life might be made perpetual by repeat listens to Kanye's music, thus ensuring the longevity of his career, but we had yet to get over that initial hurdle.

The fearsome quest had begun when Kanye and I were students at the Chicago State University in Illinois, vividly conscious for the first time of the thoroughly anemic nature of the mainstream hip-hop scene. That was years ago, but Kanye looked scarcely a day older now — he was well-groomed, well-dressed, soft-voiced, and introspective, with only an occasional flash of temper (usually on Twitter) to tell of the hardening and growing fanaticism of his character under the pressure of his terrible investigations. Our experiences had often been hideous in the extreme; the result of subpar tracks, as when lumps of Biggie's ashes had been galvanised into morbid, unnatural, and brainless motion. The loathsome Biggie/Hug-Me/Dropout/Sewage monstrosity had clawed out of its shallow-watered grave in the toilet bowl and done a dirty deed, and Kanye had had to shoot the creature. It only took four shots to put The Notorious B.I.G. down the first time. The second time it took a full clip.

It was not easy to acquire bodies to experiment on, so in our limited experience we had created nameless horrors. It was disturbing to think that at least one of our monsters still lived — that thought haunted us shadowingly, till finally Kanye disappeared under frightful circumstances. But at the time of the recording of *808s & Heartbreak*, our fears were subordinate to Kanye's sorrow, as his beloved mother had then recently passed.

There has been much speculation in the media that Kanye was in some way to blame for his mother's death. He could have afforded to send her to the best cosmetic surgeon in the world, they reasoned, instead of that diploma-less, alcoholic, reality TV show hack. Donda West's GP had advised against the surgery, but despite his recommendation the so-called Celebrity Surgeon went ahead with it. It was reported that the day after the procedure, while she was recovering at Kanye's home, Donda had collapsed and was rushed to the hospital. She was pronounced dead on arrival. But the events that transpired that day differ substantially from this account.

I had been on a long visit to my parents in Illinois at the time, fielding the usual questions about a man my age not being married, and upon my return for the funeral found Kanye in a state of what could only be described as optimistic grief. He had, he told me excitedly, in all likelihood solved the problem of track freshness through an approach from an entirely new angle — that of Auto-Tuned singing. I had known that he was working on a new album, and was not surprised to hear that it was going well; but until he explained the details I was rather puzzled as to how such an approach could help, since the objectionable staleness of Auto-Tuned tracks was exactly the machine he had begun his career raging against. This irony, I now saw, Kanye was clearly unaware of, as he had been creating his electronica tinged tracks in a hermetic bubble, like some kind of hip-hop Tod Lubitch, trusting to the muse of his own whimsy. He said the sorrow he was feeling at the loss of his mother couldn't be conveyed through mere rapping, he needed to take a more sensitive approach. And since he couldn't actually sing for shit, he sold himself on the idea of Auto-Tune. This, he assured me, was the secret to not only the reanimation of hip-hop, but the reanimation of the dead. He cited the reanimation of Cher's career by the single "Believe" — which is widely considered to be the first commercial use of the Auto-Tune effect — and the fact that her stiff, pale features had a lifeless quality about them. He claimed he had it on good authority that Cher pioneered the technique after the death of her ex-husband, Sonny Bono, who was supposedly living a secret second life as a ski instructor.

I arrived at Kanye's home and he took me to the secret cellar laboratory where a corpse lay under a sheet. The experiment would be a landmark in our studies, he told me, and he had been awaiting my return, so that we both might share in the spectacle of his genius. Because genius required spectacles, he said, preferably of the shutter shade variety.

Kanye then regaled me with the tale of how he had obtained the specimen. It had been a vivacious human being; a person near and dear to his heart who had been visiting with him on that occasion. The person was in the middle of a convalescence and their heart had become greatly overtaxed.

They had refused to go to the emergency room, and had suddenly collapsed only a moment later. The body, as might be expected, seemed to Kanye a heaven-sent gift. In a brief conversation before their passing, the person had made it clear that they believed in Kanye's work and wanted to posthumously contribute to it. When he politely declined, they practically begged Kanye to give them another chance at life. Who was he to say no? If this person could not be restored, no one would learn of our experiment. We would simply report the death, which was natural, to the authorities. If, on the other hand, the person could be restored, our (but mostly his) fame would be brilliantly established. Kanye hoped at last to obtain what he had never obtained before — a rekindled spark of reason and perhaps a normal, living creature.

So on that dreadful night, Kanye and I stood in the cellar laboratory and gazed at a white-sheeted figure bathed in fluorescent light. I stared fascinatedly at the sturdy frame which lay before us. I ventured to touch the arm beneath the sheet. It was still supple, pliant, yielding to my touch. I was moved to seek Kanye's assurance that the thing was truly dead. This assurance he gave readily enough, reminding me that the subject was only recently deceased. At this point a horrible thought began to form in my mind. I demanded he remove the sheet. He did so with a flourish, like an illusionist performing a trick, and my suspicions were confirmed. There on the table lay the body of his dead mother.

It took more than a little to calm me down. After repeatedly assuring me it was what his mother wanted he went to fetch a bottle of Hennessy to subdue me. "What was the harm?" he asked. We were only going to play her a little music. If it didn't work we had done nothing wrong. But if it did, we'd be famous and he'd have his beloved mother back.

There was nothing I could say to dissuade him. I could only sit and watch as he inserted the cable into his mother's lifeless arm and pressed play on "Love Lockdown." A gentle tremor seemed to affect the dead limbs, although it could have just been the warble of the Auto-Tune. Kanye nodded to the beat and sang along off-key under his breath. I thought it an odd choice of song, as lyrically the love being expressed was not the love shared between a mother and son. At least not normally. But as I had learned throughout the years, Kanye was anything but normal.

I cannot express the wild, breathless suspense with which we waited for results on this most important of specimens — the first we could reasonably expect to open its lips in rational speech, perhaps to tell of what it had seen beyond the unfathomable abyss.

Kanye's mother had raised him a Christian, believing in the soul and attributing all the working of consciousness to a higher power; consequently he looked for revelation of secrets from gulfs and caverns beyond death's barrier. I did not wholly disagree with him theoretically. I too held vague instinctive remnants of the primitive faith of my forefathers; so that I could not help eyeing the corpse with a certain amount of awe and terrible expectation. Besides — I could not extract from my memory that hideous, inhuman shriek we heard on the night we conducted our first experiment in the deserted farmhouse near Spahn Ranch.

Very little time had elapsed before I saw the attempt was not to be a total failure. A touch of pink came to cheeks hitherto lacking warmth, and spread out under the decedent's ample chin. Kanye, who had his hand on the pulse of the left wrist, nodded significantly. There followed a few spasmodic muscular motions, and then an audible breathing and visible motion of the chest. Kanye watched the heave of the generous bosom with the nostalgia of a weaned child. I looked at the closed eyelids, and thought I detected a quivering. Then the lids opened, shewing eyes which were grey, calm, and alive, but still unintelligent and not even curious.

In a moment of fantastic whim I whispered questions to the reddening ears; questions of other worlds of which the memory might still be present. Subsequent terror drove them from my mind, but I think the last one, which I repeated, was: "Where have you been?" I do not yet know whether I was answered or not, for no sound came from the well-shaped mouth; but I do know that at that moment I firmly thought the plump lips moved silently, forming syllables which I would have vocalised as "only one" if that phrase had possessed any sense or relevancy at the time. At that moment, as I say, I was elated with the conviction that the one great goal had been attained; and that for the first time a reanimated corpse had uttered distinct words impelled by actual reason. Kanye and I embraced with glee.

In the next moment there was no doubt about the triumph; no doubt that Kanye's music had truly accomplished, at least temporarily, its full mission of restoring rational and articulate life to the dead. But in that triumph there came to me the greatest of all horrors — not horror of the thing that spoke, but of the deed that I had witnessed and of the man with whom my professional fortunes were joined.

For that very body, at last writhing into full and terrifying consciousness with eyes dilated at the memory of its last scene on earth, threw out its frantic hands in a life and death struggle with the air, and suddenly collapsing into a second and final dissolution from which there could be no return, screamed out the cry that will ring eternally in my aching brain:

"Kanye! What are you doing? Keep off, you accursed little fiend — keep that damned pillow away from my face!"

V. The Horror of the Hova

Many rappers have related hideous things in their music; events which took place on the streets of the Bronx or the city of Compton. Some of these things have made me faint, others have convulsed me with devastating nausea, while still others have made me tremble and look over my shoulder in the dark; yet despite the worst of them I believe I can myself relate the most hideous thing of all — the shocking, the unnatural, the unbelievable horror of Jay-Z and Kanye's falling out.

The incident with his mother had put Kanye off his Frankenstein-like experiments for a while. The publicity cycle for *808s & Heartbreak* wound down and things got back to normal — normal for Kanye, that is. He shot his mouth off at the MTV Music Awards, cancelled a tour with Lady Gaga, and retreated to a Hawaii recording studio to lick his wounds. He threw himself into fashion, and fashion threw him right back out. He released *My Beautiful Dark Twisted Fantasy*, collaborated with Jay-Z on *Watch the Throne*, and released the *Cruel Summer* compilation on his own GOOD Music record label. I was his constant companion through it all and I have to say, he seemed to be making good on his promise to reanimate hip-hop. I had never seen him so focused. Our bond was stronger than ever.

Then Kimye happened.

Not even Kanye's Auto-Tuneless performance of "Love Lockdown" on *Saturday Night Live* was more wretched than the dolorous lament of my soul. His bromance with mentor Jay-Z I could handle, dalliances with aspiring starlets, fine — but this… this was not good. Kanye had spent his whole career trying to perpetuate the image of a brilliant artist, but by shacking up with that tabloid queen, whose career was a causal loop of fame for fame's sake, and proclaiming her his "Perfect Bitch," he was undermining the ideals he had strived so hard to espouse.

Almost immediately I was pushed aside, relegated to clandestine work in the studio while Kanye and Kim tried to take over the world like a pair of genetically enhanced laboratory mice. It was a lonely time for me, although I was relieved that the only life Kanye was attempting to create was in a Kardashian womb, unappealing as that may be. In fact, it wasn't long before he proclaimed himself an expectant father to a sold out crowd in Atlantic City. The next day, this was confirmed by Kim on her personal blog.

I have to say, North West was the only good thing to come out of this whole charade. I took to that little bundle of boogers almost immediately. When Kanye would bring her to the studio I would play the role of dutiful babysitter. Although a very public campaign was run by Kim's friend Jonathan Cheban, and most people suspected it would be Jay-Z, I became the child's de facto godfather. I paid more attention to her than her own parents, who were constantly preoccupied with their careers. In fact, I was the one who discovered little Nori was a polydactyly. She was two months old at the time and neither of her self-indulgent parents had noticed she possessed an extra toe on her left foot (although to be fair, I don't think either of them can count very well).

As I said, at a certain point it looked like Jay-Z was going to be named Nori's godfather, but that all changed after the wedding. Frankly, the event was disgusting. An orgiastic display of narcissism and gluttony that would make George R. R. Martin cringe. Dubbed the #WORLDSMOSTTALKED-ABOUTWEDDING by the Internet, it (allegedly, as I was not on the guest list) featured anatomically correct nude statues of the bride and groom, a fifty-foot tall golden box that housed the rest rooms, each of which contained its own full-service bar; marble seating arrangements in which the guests' names were carved, the majority of which were misspelled; a custom built marble piano that even Elton John would have considered tacky; Jaden Smith running around dressed as "White Batman"; a crazed Justin Bieber fan who crashed the wedding and fell off the golden toilet house; a chorus of blind, gelded orphans who sang "Hava Nagila" during the processional; and a fifteen liter Nebuchadnezzar sized bottle of Chianti dipped in gold with a fifty carat diamond cork, an extravagant gift from Beyonce and Jay-Z, who pulled a no-show.

If you thought zip-lining and Super Bowls made Kanye sad, the absence of his mentor at his wedding was devastating. The duo had previously weathered the perceived (by Kanye) slight of "Death of Auto-Tune", the lead single from Jay-Z's *The Blueprint 3*; as well as Jay-Z dropping an Auto-

Tuned collaboration produced by Kanye from the same album; but the wedding snub caused a chasm sized rift between the two — or, in the parlance of our times, a "beef." In retaliation, Kanye omitted numerous shoutouts to HOV from his songs during performances in Austin and Bonnaroo. He also went on a long-winded rant where he was quoted as saying, "Ain't no bitch gonna pull that Solange 'ish on me," a reference to the infamous elevator dustup between Jigga and his sister-in-law.

Here it must be said that Jay-Z was nothing but a gentleman during the entire ordeal, and did his best to make amends with his irate friend. It was Jay who extended the oily olive branch of reconciliation to the temperamental rapper and initiated peace talks. At the time we were in pre-production on album seven, and Kanye had invited Jay-Z over to listen to some tracks. He was excited because he had been collaborating with a true living legend — Sir Paul McCartney of The Beatles (Google it, kids) — and wanted to rub it in HOV's face. Little did Jay know what the unlikely duo had planned. Little did I, for that matter.

McCartney was getting on in years, and realized that although his music would most likely live forever in the annals of history, his body would not.

Unbeknownst to me, Kanye had been talking up his reanimation techniques with the famous Beatle and McCartney's interest was well piqued. It was to be Kanye's crowning achievement: by joining forces with one of the greatest musicians of all time he was guaranteed to produce music so fantastic it would give life to the dead. It was Sir Paul's hope that this technique would be perfected by the time he shuffled off this mortal coil. That way he would be sure to win the last living Beatle contest over Ringo.

As soon as Jay entered the studio a colossal struggle ensued. Sir Paul was a feeble old git, but it was two against one. Sure, there were reasons why I could have separated the three; especially since I had begun to find the practice of recording with and the companionship of Kanye more and more irritating; but I could not resist the imperious curiosity of what might possibly transpire.

When I say Kanye was shit in a fight, I do not mean to imply that he was a pussy, anxious for the safety of his own person. Always the hothead — slight, moody, starry-eyed, and ambitious — I think he secretly sneered at my occasional lack of enthusiasm for machismo and my displays of supine neutrality. However, when he wanted something, he did anything in his power to achieve it. And what he wanted was not a thing which many persons want, but something connected with the peculiar road less traveled which he had chosen quite clandestinely to follow, and in which he had achieved amazing and occasionally hideous results.

Kanye needed bodies to achieve his life-work of reanimating the dead. This work was not known to the throngs of acolytic fans who had so swiftly built up his fame after he dropped out of college; but was only too well known to me, who had been his closest friend (some would say too close) and sole companion since the old days at Chicago State University. It was in those days that he had begun his life's work, first in the musical realm and then on human bodies shockingly obtained. He inserted a cable into the veins of dead things, and if the tracks he played were fresh enough the bodies responded in strange ways. He had had much trouble in discovering the proper mix, for each person was found to have its own personal musical tastes. Terror stalked him when he reflected on his partial failures; nameless things resulting from inferior musical arrangements or from bodies insufficiently disposed of. A certain number of these failures had remained alive — one was in a mental health facility while others had vanished — and as he thought of

conceivable yet virtually impossible eventualities
he often flew into fear-rage.

Kanye had soon learned that absolute freshness
was the prime requisite for life-giving music, and
had accordingly resorted to frightful and unnatural
expedients in body-snatching. In college and
during our early days together, my attitude toward
him had been largely one of fascinated admiration;
but as his boldness in methods grew, I began to
develop a gnawing fear. I did not like the way he
looked at healthy living bodies. At first I thought it
was mere jealousy. Then there came a nightmarish
session in an L.A. recording studio where I learned
that a certain specimen — his own beloved mother,
in fact — had been a living body when he secured
it. That was the first time he had ever been able to
revive the quality of rational thought in a corpse;
and his success, obtained at such a loathsome cost,
had completely hardened him.

Of his methods in the intervening years I dare
not speak. I was held to him by sheer force of
loyalty, and witnessed sights that no human tongue
could repeat. Gradually I came to find Kanye
himself more horrible than anything he did — that
was when it dawned on me that his once normal
musical zeal for reanimating hip-hop had subtly

transformed into a morbid and ghoulish curiosity and secret sense of charnel megalomania. His interest became a hellish and perverse addiction to the repellently and fiendishly abnormal; he gloated calmly over artificial monstrosities which would make most healthy men drop dead from fright and disgust; he became, behind his pallid intellectuality, a fastidious Bukowski of physical experiment — a languid Erick Sermon of the grave.

Dangers he met unflinchingly; crimes he committed unmoved. I think the climax came when he had proved his point that the glory of hip-hop could be restored, and had sought new worlds to conquer by experimenting on the reanimation of dead bodies. He had wild and original ideas on the independent music scene and vital properties of mainstream radio; and achieved some hideous preliminary results in the form of reanimated husks. All this research work required a prodigious supply of fresh music and deceased human flesh. It was the stress involved in the latter's procurement that caused Kanye to become so unpredictable in his behaviour.

The phantasmal, unmentionable thing which I am about to mention occurred late one night not long after Kanye's marriage to Kim Kardashian, in a private studio at his home in LA. I wonder even now if it could have been other than a horrific dream of delirium. There he worked like a butcher in the midst of his gory wares, cutting and pasting tracks in his laptop. I could never get used to the nonchalance with which he handled such situations. At times he actually did perform marvels of musical ingenuity; but his chief delights were of a less public and philanthropic kind, requiring many explanations to the neighbors of sounds which seemed peculiar even in light of his most experimental recordings. Among these sounds were frequent gunshots, and, just once, the barely intelligible exclamation, *PUTTINONTHERITZ!* (Kanye never forgave me for downloading that Taco album on his personal iTunes account.)

Looking back I should have seen it coming. Jay-Z was a splendid specimen — a man at once physically powerful and of such high musical standards that a receptive nervous system was assured. It was rather ironic, for he was the man who had mentored Kanye, and now he was destined to be the subject of his greatest experiment. Moreover, he had in the past been privy to the theory of reanimation to some extent under Kanye.

Jay-Z showed up in a bulletproof limousine, his preferred mode of transportation, so it made no sense for Kanye and Paul to ambush him upon arrival. They waited until he entered the studio. The attack was both spectacular and awful; Kanye struck the first blow by smashing Jay-Z over the head with his framed Platinum record for *808s & Heartbreak*. Jay-Z was dazed, but having a good six inches on Kanye and a longer reach, soon obtained the upper hand in the grappling that followed. That was when Sir Paul joined the fray.

In a dark corner of the studio, Kanye had kept a full-size replica of the sword from George Condo's cover art for the "Power" single, which ended in a crowned, papier-mâché bust of the rapper's own head, like some Arthurian sword in the stone. It was this implement the charging Beatle wielded, Kanye head and all. It was too horrific. I had to turn away.

Jay-Z was unrecognisable afterward. The sword itself was blunt and McCartney not very strong, but the havoc yielded up the great rapper in a nearly decapitated but otherwise intact condition. Kanye had greedily seized the lifeless thing which had once been his friend and fellow-rapper; and I shuddered when he took the dull blade from Paul and finished severing the head, placing it on its own dissecting tray, and proceeded to treat the decapitated body on the operating table. He inserted the music cable into the neck stump and covered the ghastly aperture with duct tape. I knew what he wanted — to see if this highly organised body could exhibit, without its head, any of the signs of the mental life which had distinguished Jay-Z. Once the mentor of Kanye, this silent trunk was now gruesomely called upon to exemplify the mad genius' work.

I can still see Kanye under the sinister fluorescent lights, a bloody bootprint stamped across his face, as he leaned over the body of his friend and said, "Auto-Tune isn't dead, motherfucker. You are," and pressed play on "Only One", featuring keys by Paul. An eerie calm descended upon the gore-splattered studio. John Lennon must have been rolling in his grave, for there was madness in that room. For only madness could account for such supremely talented people producing such a shitty song.

Jay-Z, as Kanye repeatedly observed, had a splendid musical pedigree. Much was expected of his headless corpse; and as a few twitching motions began to appear, I could see the feverish interest on Kanye's face. He was ready, I think, to see proof of his increasingly strong opinion that consciousness, reason, and personality can exist independently of the brain — that music could function as man's central connective spirit. The body is merely a machine of nervous matter, each section more or less complete in itself. In one triumphant demonstration Kanye was about to relegate the mystery of life to the category of myth. The body twitched more vigorously, and beneath our avid eyes commenced to heave in a frightful way. The arms stirred disquietingly, the scrotum drew up, and various muscles contracted in a repulsive kind of writhing. Then the headless thing threw out its arms in a gesture which was unmistakably one of desperation — an intelligent desperation apparently sufficient to prove every one of Kanye's theories. Certainly, the nerves were recalling Jay-Z's last act in life; the struggle to get free of Kanye West and Paul McCartney.

What followed, I shall never positively know. It may have been wholly an hallucination from the shock caused at that instant as the entire recording studio went up in flames — in the excitement of the preceding melee, Kanye had forgotten about the pumpkin flavored Toaster Strudel he had put in the toaster oven and a cataclysmic electrical fire ensued — but who can gainsay, since Kanye and I were the only proved survivors? Kanye wanted to believe it was an hallucination, but there were times when he could not; for it was queer that we both had the same exact experience. The hideous occurrence itself was very simple, notable only for what it implied.

The body on the table had risen with a blind and terrible groping, and we had heard a sound. I should not call that sound a voice, for it was too awful. And yet its timbre was not the most awful thing about it. For it had come from the decapitated head that sat on the dissecting tray in the corner.

"I am Godzilla of these favelas, new God flow!" the awful thing shouted.

VI. Legions in Paris

When Kanye West disappeared, the police questioned me closely. They suspected that I was holding something back, and perhaps suspected graver things; but I could not tell them the truth because they would not have believed it. They knew, indeed, that Kanye had been connected with activities beyond the jackassery of ordinary men, such as publicly accusing the President of the United States of not caring about black people. As true as that sentiment might have been, a charity relief benefit was not the most appropriate forum in which to voice it. Then there were his hideous experiments in the reanimation of dead bodies, which had long been too extensive to admit of perfect secrecy. But the final soul-shattering catastrophe held elements of daemoniac phantasy (and Damonic fantasy) which make even me doubt the reality of what I saw.

I was Kanye's closest friend and confidential assistant. Some would say too close, and too confidential. We had met years before, in college, and from the first I had shared in his terrible researches. He had slowly tried to perfect a song which, when plugged directly into the veins of the deceased, would restore life; a labour demanding an abundance of fresh music and access to corpses, therefore involving the most unnatural actions. Still more shocking were the products of some of the attempts — grisly masses of flesh previously dead that Kanye waked to a blind, brainless, nauseous animation.

This need for corpses had been Kanye's moral undoing. They were hard to get, and one awful day he had secured a specimen while it was still alive and vigorous—his own mother. A struggle, a pillow, and an Auto-Tuned track transformed the corpse, and the experiment had succeeded for a brief and memorable moment; but Kanye had emerged with a soul calloused and seared, and a hardened eye for potential specimens. Toward the last I became acutely afraid of him, for he began to look at me that way. People noticed and misconstrued his glances, and after his disappearance used that as a basis for some absurd assumptions about the nature of our relationship.

Kanye, in reality, was more afraid than I; for his abominable pursuits entailed a life of furtiveness and dread of every shadow. Partly it was the paparazzi he feared, for they were always snooping about, waiting to expose his every secret for personal gain. Yet sometimes his nervousness was deeper and more nebulous, touching on certain indescribable things into which he had injected a morbid life, and from which he had not seen that life depart. He usually finished his experiments with a nine-millimeter, as he did with Biggie, but a few times he had not been quick enough. There was that first specimen whose car was later found empty, and the reanimated Damon Dash, who was thrust unidentified into a padded cell where he beat the walls for over a decade.

In saying that Kanye's fear of his specimens was nebulous, I have in mind particularly its complex nature. Part of it came merely from knowing of the existence of such nameless monsters, while another part arose from apprehension of the bodily harm they might under certain circumstances do him. Their disappearance added horror to the situation — of them all, Kanye knew the whereabouts of only one, the pitiful Damon Dash thing. Then there was a more subtle fear — a very fantastic sensation resulting from a curious experiment shortly after his wedding to Kim Kardashian. Kanye, with the help of Sir Paul McCartney, one of the most venerable musicians of all time, had decapitated his mentor and friend, Jay-Z, and reanimated the head and body separately. Jay-Z was the only person besides me who knew about Kanye's experiments and could have duplicated them. The head had been removed in the fray, still the possibilities of quasi-intelligent life in the trunk had to be investigated. Just as the studio caught fire there had been a success. The trunk had moved intelligently, and, unbelievable to relate, we were both sickeningly sure that articulate sounds had come from the detached head as it lay in a shadowy corner of the laboratory. The fire had been merciful, in a way — but Kanye could never feel as certain as he wished, that we two were the only survivors. He used to make shuddering conjectures about the possible actions of a headless rapper with the power of reanimating the dead and his elderly English sidekick.

Kanye's latest quarters were in an apartment of much elegance in Paris, overlooking the river below. He had chosen the place for a purely symbolic and fantastically aesthetic reason — that reason being a particularly inspiring Corbusier lamp. The recording studio was in the living room, but the ancient building had a secret sub-cellar that contained a huge incinerator for the quiet and complete disposal of such bodies, or fragments and synthetic mockeries of bodies, as might remain from the morbid experiments and unhallowed amusements of the owner.

During the excavation of this cellar the workmen had struck some exceedingly ancient masonry connected to the local cemetery. I was with Kanye when he studied the nitrous, dripping walls laid bare by the spades and mattocks of the men, and was prepared for the gruesome thrill which would attend the uncovering of centuried grave-secrets; but for the first time Kanye's timidity conquered his temerity, and he betrayed his degenerating moral fibre by ordering the masonry left intact and plastered over. Thus it remained till that final hellish night; part of the walls of the secret laboratory. Kanye was known for his decadence — the extravagant wedding, his penchant for disposable alligator underwear, the shameless pillaging of imagery from Alejandro Jodorowsky — but I must add that these were purely part of his exterior life. Inwardly he was the same to the last

— cold, calculating, with a general aspect of youth which years and fears seemed never to change. Although a word not often associated with Kanye, I'd go as far as saying he seemed calm, even when he thought of that bohemian's abandoned car; even when he thought of the carnivorous Damon Dash that gnawed and pawed at padded walls.

The end of Kanye West began one evening in our joint study when he was dividing his curious glance between the newspaper and me. A strange headline item had struck at him from the crumpled pages, and an icy claw had seemed to reach down through the years to grip his sagging balls. Something fearsome and incredible had happened back at the mental health facility in L.A., stunning the neighbourhood and baffling the police. In the small hours of the morning a body of silent men had entered the grounds, and their leader had aroused the attendants. He was a menacing figure who talked without moving his lips and whose voice seemed almost ventriloquially connected with an immense black box he carried. His expressionless face had striking features and piercing eyes, but had shocked the superintendent when the hall light fell on it — for it was made of papier-mâché. A slight Englishman in a Canadian tuxedo playing an acoustic guitar guided his steps; a repellent little imp whose leathery face was scarred beyond recognition. The speaker had asked for the custody of the cannibal monster that was Damon Dash, committed years before; and upon being refused, gave a signal which precipitated a shocking riot. The fiends had beaten, trampled, and bitten every attendant who did not flee; killing four and finally succeeding in the liberation of the monster. Those victims who could recall the event without hysteria swore that the creatures had acted less like men than like unthinkable automata guided by the paper-faced leader. By the time help could be summoned, every trace of the men and of their mad charge had vanished.

From the hour of reading this item until midnight, Kanye sat almost paralysed. At midnight the doorbell rang, startling him fearfully. Kanye never answered his own door, it was something he had hired street urchins to do, but they had all been sent home for the evening so the task fell to me. As I have told the police, there was no vehicle in the street, but only a group of strange-looking figures bearing a large black box which they deposited in the hallway after one of them had grunted in an effeminate British voice, "Express — prepaid. And

P.S., I love you. You you *you*." He jabbed his finger at me as he emphasized the final "you." It felt like a threat.

The group filed out of the house with a jerky tread, and as I watched them go I had an odd idea that they were turning toward the cemetery on which the back of the apartment abutted. When I slammed the door after them Kanye came downstairs and looked at the box. It was about two feet square, and bore Kanye's correct name and present address. It also bore the inscription, "From Shawn Corey Carter." A few years before, in Kanye's home studio, a freak strudel accident had caused an electrical fire that destroyed the headless reanimated trunk of Jay-Z, as well as the detached head which — perhaps — had uttered articulate sounds.

Kanye did not get worked up into one of his patented hissy-fits. His condition was more ghastly. Quickly he said, "It's the finish. Let's incinerate it." We carried the thing down to the basement — listening. I do not remember many particulars — you can imagine my state of mind — but it is a vicious lie to say it was Kanye's body which I put into the incinerator. We both inserted the whole unopened wooden box, closed the door, and started the machine. No sound came from within the box.

It was Kanye who first noticed the falling plaster on that part of the wall where the ancient tomb masonry had been covered up. I was going to run, but he stopped me. Then I saw a small black aperture, felt a ghoulish wind of ice, and smelled the charnel bowels of a putrescent earth. There was no sound, but just then the lights went out and I saw outlined against some phosphorescence of the nether world a horde of silent toiling things which only insanity — or Kanye West — could create. Their outlines were human, semi-human, fractionally human, and not human at all — the horde was grotesquely heterogeneous. It was a scene straight out of Kanye's controversial "Monster" video. They were removing the stones quietly, one by one, from the centuried wall. And then, as the breach became large enough, they came out into the laboratory in single file; led by a thing with a head made of papier-mâché. The mad-eyed Dash monstrosity stepped out from behind the leader. The young Bohemian did the same. They both seized Kanye by the arm. Kanye did not resist. He simply nodded at the papier-mâché man. "Jay," he said to him. Despite not having eyes to see, the man nodded back. It must have been like looking into a mirror. A mirror with a papier-mâché reflection.

Then they all sprang at him and tore him to pieces before my eyes, bearing the fragments away into that subterranean vault of fabulous abominations. Kanye's head was carried off by the paper-headed leader. As it disappeared I saw that Kanye's dark eyes were hideously blazing with frantic, visible emotion.

The building superintendent found me unconscious in the morning. Kanye was gone. The incinerator contained only unidentifiable ashes. Detectives have questioned me, but what can I say? The Damon Dash tragedy they will not connect with Kanye; not that, nor the men with the box, whose existence they deny. I told them of the vault, and they pointed to the unbroken plaster wall and laughed. So I told them no more. They imply that I am either a madman or a murderer — perhaps it was a crime of passion, they said. I told them I did not appreciate the insinuation, which was in especially poor taste considering recent events.

I live a simpler life now, one of unbroken solitude. As was expected, the bulk of Kanye's fortune went to his daughter, but he was kind enough to set aside a small endowment for his former friend and companion. He had been well endowed, and was always extremely generous with those endowments. Sometimes I wonder if he is truly dead and gone, the horrific events of that night becoming harder to recall with each passing year. Or maybe this whole "Kanye is dead" thing is a publicity trick he picked up from McCartney. From time to time there are whispers in the press — a paper-faced man spotted at a fashion show, the modern-day equivalent of an Elvis sighting — but nothing substantial. Kim Kardashian has teamed up with Voletta Wallace to produce Kanye's first album of posthumous material — I received the press release only yesterday. It is entitled *Through the Box*, and the cover art consists of a simple black construction with six square sides, three of which meet at each vertex. The titular first single will be released in a month's time. Kanye had a treasure trove of unreleased material, but it is not a track I am familiar with. There is so much I can't remember these days. Still, I can't shake that familiar feeling of dread lurking just around the corner…

About the Author

Joshua Chaplinsky is the Managing Editor of LitReactor.com. He has also written for popular film site TwitchFilm and for ChuckPalahniuk.net, the official website of 'Fight Club' author Chuck Palahniuk. His short fiction has/will appear in *Zetetic*, *Motherboard*, *Dark Moon Digest*, *L'allure des Mots*, *Pantheon Magazine*, *Fabula Argentea*, and *Crack the Spine*. More info at joshuachaplinsky.com.

CPSIA information can be obtained at www.ICGtesting.com
Printed in the USA
BVOW08s1320080916

461411BV00029B/17/P

9 780692 516126